# Yahweh Publication Presents

# CHAPTERS OF LIFE

Ginny Mukesh Jain

Yahweh Publication

Tamilnadu, India



yahweh_publication

Yahweh Publication

yahwehpublication@gmail.com

✆ 9363734705

*Your words, our passion!*

Yahweh Publication proudly presents,

Chapters of life.

ISBN: 978-81-991357-9-6.

First edition: 2025 August.

Compiled by: Ginny Mukesh Jain.

Cover design: Yahweh Publication.

Book formatting: Yahweh Publication.

# Disclaimer

This book, Chapters of life, is a work of fiction. All names, characters and incidents portrayed in this book are either a product of the author's imagination or are used factiously. Any resemblance to actual persons, living or dead, or actual events is purely coincidental.

Every effort has been made to ensure the accuracy and integrity of the material after obtaining the writer's consent. However, the authors and Yahweh Publication declaim any liability for any loss, damage or disruption caused by errors of omissions, whether resulting from negligence, accident or any other cause. Yahweh Publication endeavors to present error-free content, but we do not assume responsibility for any inadvertent mistakes. In cases of plagiarism, sole responsibility lies with the co-authors; the publisher disclaims liability.

This book is a product of Yahweh Publication's dedicated efforts. Yahweh Publication and compilers bear no responsibility for any plagiarized co tent. Only co-authors are accountable in the event of plagiarism. It is important to note that this book does not intend to disrespect any community, caste, religion, creed, nationality or gender.

- *R. Malin Jenifer.*
- *Founder & CEO.*

# Acknowledgement

Thanking the entire team of Yahweh Publication for trusting on me and giving me a chance to publish my beloved anthology.

Secondly all thanks to all the wonderful co-authors for their patience and hard work throughout the anthology.

This anthology is a truest attempt to share all the emotions one goes through in life and hence this anthology is named as 'Chapters of Life'.

May this anthology become a power for every reader to accept their own emotions during various chapters of life!!

- *Ginny Mukesh Jain.*

# About the book

The anthology named 'Chapters of life' typically revolves around the various emotions we feel throughout our lives.

In this anthology many co-authors across the world have shared their own feelings towards chapters of life. This is basically an anthology that will specifically refer to the emotions people faces when they went through certain situations in life. In simpler words, it is a combined mixture of sweet and sour, happy and sad.

Read this book and enjoy. Thank you!

- *Ginny Mukesh Jain.*

# FOUNDER AND CEO OF YAHWEH PUBLICATION

## Mrs. R. Malin Jenifer

Mrs. R. Malin Jenifer, daughter of Mr. M. Raja & Mrs. R. Beula and wife of Mr. Martin Manoah. She is a mother of two kids. And, she is an optimistic and energetic person with a big dream from a small town in Ooty. She is a post graduate in Biochemistry and she holds a Diploma in Bio-informatics. Though she is a life science graduate, her interest towards art and literature made her a writer. She has worked as an Online tutor and an assistant professor at different organizations. She is the person who is basically an extrovert and selectively an introvert. She strongly believes in the destination and karma. And, her hope relies on the patience and hard-work. As a follower of Christ, she has a strong belief in a Bible verse *(Phil 4:13)* that says, *'I can do all the things through Christ which strengtheneth me'* and she completely trusts the word and plan of God. She believes that her day starts with the blessings of Christ and ends at his feet. She is a kind of straightforward. She owns a publication unit named 'Yahweh Publication'. She is the person who seeks for the recognition for her work and she believes that this publication is the first step of it. And currently, she is playing roles like writer, compiler and project head under different publications.

She can be contacted through her mail yahwehpublication@gmail.com and her Instagram handle: yahweh_publication.

# Compiler

## Ginny Mukesh Jain

Ginny Mukesh Jain, a passionate writer, is on a heartfelt journey of literary creation. With a deep love for the written word, she aspires to construct a world of writings that encapsulate her emotions and joys. Her writing endeavors are not only a personal dream but also a way to honor the dreams of my parents.

She is dedicated to crafting relatable stories that resonate with readers. Writing is not just a passion but a daily dream that she ardently pursues. The encouraging comments and feedback from readers serve as the radiant sunshine that brightens her every day.

After a while,

You'll finally learn

The sober difference between,

Holding a hand and chasing a soul,

And you'll simply learn that love doesn't always mean loving and

Company doesn't always mean comfort zone.

And you'll simply know,

That kisses aren't contracts

And present moments aren't always promises for future.

And you'll simply know,

That you're really worth,

You're really strong,

And you can heal alone.

With every goodbye, you'll learn.

- *Gin.*

तुम याद रखोगे तो मैं निशानी हूँ
और अगर तुम भूल जाओगे तो मैं एक कहानी हूँ,
चेहरा देखोगे तो हस्ती हुई ही नज़र आऊँगी
लेकिन अगर दिल झाकोंगे तो टूटी हुई नज़र आऊँगी,
सबको प्यार देने की आदत है मुझे
कोई मुझे कितना भी दुख दे-दे
उसके लिए मेरे दिल में फिर भी इज़्ज़त है,
लाख कोशिश की लेकिन कोई समझ नहीं पाया
हाँ, मैं उलझी हुई ज़िंदगानी हूँ।

- *Gin.*

ज़िंदगी एक सवाल सी बन गई है
जिसका जवाब मिलता नहीं है,
आस-पास शोर तो बहुत है
लेकिन उसकी आवाज़ें कानों तक पहुँचती नहीं है।

ज़िक्र भी मत कर
फ़िक्र भी मत कर,
तू सिर्फ़ तेरे जज़्बातों कि कद्र कर
और तेरा वक़्त आने का इंतज़ार कर।

इतना पास आकर समझाया था उसने,
की दूर कैसे जाते है वो तो पता ही नहीं!
दिल पर लगी बातें,
अक्सर आवाज छीन लेती है।

- *Gin.*

# Authors

1. Aashim Sharma
2. Aditi Sharma
3. Author Charu
4. Debjani Padhi
5. Disha Choudhary
6. Disha Shah
7. Dr. Major Nalini Janardhanan
8. Dr. Richa Biswal
9. Dr. Rutam Biswal
10. Dr. Satwik Chatterjee
11. Ishani Ganguly
12. Kajal Sahu
13. Karan Dhingra
14. Kirti Verma
15. Mayank Kumar
16. Mr. Saroj Kumar Ojha
17. Pradnya-Athreya Narawade
18. Pranali Vijay Patil
19. R. Jayaprakash
20. Rangeesh Chandrasekar

21. Reem Sayed
22. Santhosh Kumar R J
23. Shivangi Jaiswal
24. Shroddha Mukherjee
25. Simran Thapa
26. Shruti Samskruti
27. Suraj Kumar
28. Tarun Kaushik
29. Vansh Sharma
30. Wolfie

# Co-author
# Aashim Sharma

He is Aashim Sharma. He is a poet, story teller, singer and guitarist by hobby. He can write in four languages Hindi, Punjabi, English and Urdu. He is from Punjab.

# Emotions of life

In the cradle of breath, where moments are born,
Life writes its verses on pages well-worn.
Not just in heartbeats, or in silent strife,
But in the soul's song — the emotions of life.

Joy bursts forth like a midsummer light,
Spilling its gold on the darkest of night.
A child's laughter, a victory's flame,
A whisper of love when you hear your name.

Sadness drips slow, like rain on the glass,
Moments of longing that silently pass.
A photo, a farewell, a once-said word,
The ache of a truth that goes unheard.

Hope is a lantern in tunnels so deep,
That dances awake when we try to sleep.
It sings in the silence, it fights through despair,
A fragile but fearless breath in the air.

Anger is fire, fierce and wild,
The storm inside the tender child.
It shakes the walls, it scars the skies,
Yet clears the clouds when truth replies.

Love is the ocean — wide and vast,
It holds the future, heals the past.
It dwells in touches, in tears that shine,
In letting go, in drawing the line.

Fear is the shadow that walks behind,
Whispering lies to the wandering mind.
It cages the bird, it dims the light,
Yet dies when faced in the arms of night.

Gratitude blooms in the humblest place,
In a stranger's smile, a kind embrace.
It teaches the soul to softly kneel,
And honor the small things we often feel.

Loneliness echoes in crowded rooms,
In busy streets and bright costumes.
It sits in silence, it sighs in songs,
It longs for where a heart belongs.

Wonder dances in a child's wide eyes,
In stardust dreams and painted skies.
It asks no why, it needs no proof,
It lives in stories and ancient truth.

Regret is a clock that won't unwind,
A haunting hush inside the mind.
It teaches lessons, sharp and slow,
Of things unsaid, and seeds we sow.

Peace arrives not in the end,
But in the moment, round the bend.
In quiet tea, or sacred air,
In letting go, in being there.

Forgiveness breathes when grudges die,
When pride steps back and lets truth lie.
It frees the heart, it lifts the weight,
It gives the soul a cleaner slate.

Passion burns with crimson flame,
It shouts with purpose, carves your name.
It drives the artist, the lover, the fight,
It fuels the dreams that take their flight.

Each feeling a color, a note, a key,
In the vast symphonic mystery.
We're not just minds, or flesh and bone,
But chambers of feeling—each one our own.

So let them come, the tears and cheers,
The seasons shaped by joy and fears.
For what is life if not the art
Of feeling deeply, heart to heart?

May we rise, may we fall,
May we feel through it all.
For the measure of life is not just breath—
But the love we give
…until our death.

- *Aashim Sharma.*

## Journey of life

In every breath we take, a tide,
Of feelings swell and then subside.
Life is not just time and place -
It's every tear, each warm embrace.

The soul is stitched with threads unseen,
Of red, of gold, of blues between.
We're not machines that simply strive -
We feel our way through being alive.

---

Joy comes dancing, bright and bold,
In sunshine arms and marigold.
It laughs in circles, spins in rain,
It's found in love, and found in pain.

It's morning light on eyelids closed,
A secret kiss, a dream composed.
The way a song can make you smile,
And lift your soul for just a while.

---

Then Sorrow steps in soft and slow,
A winter wind, a silent woe.
It hums a tune of days gone by,
With heavy heart and clouded sky.

It's in goodbyes we never said,
In quiet thoughts of those long dead.
It teaches depth, it shows us grace,
And leaves its mark on every face.

---

Anger roars in crimson flame,
With clenched-up fists and pointed blame.
It's wild, raw, a burning wave,
It both destroys and dares to save.

But even fire can purify,
It strips the truth, it lights the sky.
When used with heart, not reckless might,
It stands for justice, stands for right.

---

Love - oh love, the beating core,
The tide we chase forevermore.
It builds our worlds, it breaks them too,
It's both the curse and the rescue.

It's mother's arms, it's lovers' touch,
It's poems that say far too much.
It weaves our days in threads divine,
And makes the fleeting moments shine.

---

Fear walks with us every day,
In silent doubts that cloud the way.
It grips the chest, it shakes the soul,
It's half the journey to the goal.

But courage isn't being free—
It's choosing yes when fear says flee.
For every mountain ever climbed
Was first a fear within the mind.

---

Hope is fragile, soft as mist,
But strong enough to still exist.
It flickers when the dark is near,
Yet dares to whisper, "Persevere."

A letter sent, a wish held tight,
A child still dreaming through the night.
Hope is the spark behind each tear
That says, "I'll try again next year."

---

Grief comes like a sudden tide,
No warnings left, no place to hide.
It floods the heart, it breaks the shore,
It carves a canyon at the core.

But in that depth, love lingers still,
In memories we cannot kill.
For grief is proof the love was real—
A mark of how we dared to feel.

---

Peace is soft, it does not shout,
It's what we find when storms burn out.
It waits in pauses, breath, and prayer,
In letting go, in being there.

It isn't wealth, it isn't fame—
It's knowing you are not the same.
That every joy, each hurt and strife,
Has shaped the soul that lives this life.

So feel it all—the rise, the fall,
The highs that sing, the wounds that call.
Don't numb the fire, don't cage the rain,
For life is made of joy and pain.

You are a vessel, brave and wide,
Where oceans of emotion ride.
And every tear and every grin
Is part of what you hold within.

---

The emotions of life—they come, they go,
Like winds that shape the drifting snow.
But in their dance, we come alive,
We feel, we break, we heal, we thrive.

So cry, so laugh, so scream, so sing—
For feeling is the realest thing.
Let your heart break, and beat, and burn—
That's the only way we learn.

- *Aashim Sharma.*

# Co-author

## Aditi Sharma

She is a dreamer and an achiever. Whatever she sets her eyes on, she belongs to it. Words and dance are her love language. Karan aujla for day, tears for night, Arijit for a loner. She worships the floor she walks on.

# Pretend my game

Oh! How difficult!
How difficult it is to pretend strong
When u r broken within!

How difficult it is to stop shaking your legs
When u r filled with anxiety and regrets!

How difficult it is to cover up
Everything with a smile!

And a heavy heart!

How tough is it to dance, take snaps watch movies when you are broken but trying to move on!

Why not, I'm not crying over my friend.

I'm crying upon the dream I thought which I'm going to make it true!
I imagined, I loved, and I dropped.

People think it's too easy to drop what you thought it would be.

Ask a person who gave heart and soul for it! It's never easy to move on.

We are just left with that word 'kash' at the end

While trying to be the strongest and happy person to
everyone, except your notes, nobody realised how
deeply it hits you, else they question you!
Oh! how difficult it is!

- *Aditi Sharma.*

# Hard to express

How to not express
To cry in sighs
In secret sights

How easily people
Make your fear and emotions
A weakness ..

Makes me haunt
In a night where
My tears going all way through my eyes till my chin

How difficult it seems to see
Something shattering u loved
Still accepting the fate

And we call this love
When u still desire the same thing
U loved after it betrayed you

People questioned weakness
Without knowing reasons

Butt u wish the same for that one thing
Yes ! We call this love

Note to LOVE!

Love even if u r far

U will be there on my heart till my death!
Still a hope to begin from starting stays

- *Aditi Sharma.*

# Co-author
# Charu

**Introduction** – Her name is "Charu Rana", and she is a skilled housewife. She was born March 3 on Dehradun city of Uttarakhand state.

**Experience** - Charu Rana ji has made her mark in the world of writing in just 1 year. Her works have been published in major platforms like 'Pocket Novel', 'Pratilipi', 'Story mania' and 'Lafzon Ki Kahani' app. She has contributed to the co-authorship of more than 40 books, and has compiled 3 compilations. Whose names are as follows: Struggle of Women, Selfless Love & Celebrating Two Years Of Ink And Imagination. And right now, the compilation work is going on her 5 books: Aakhri Mulakat, Aadhunik Dahej, Destiny of Love, Family &Atrangi Soulmate.

**Achievement** - Charu Rana ji's writing has received many certificates and awards. In particular, she won the third place in the "Open Challenge" competition of "Lafzon Ki Kahani" and the fourth place in the Kavita

Challenge. Her poems and stories have been published in online forums many times. A new chapter begins in Charu Rana's writing journey when her first winning short story "Kisi Ka Saath" is published in the print book "Lafzon Ki Kahani 2". She still wants to learn a lot in writing and make a name for herself through it. If you want to read her poems then she writes under the name Charu Singh in the Lafzon Ki Kahani app.

Pocket Novel App - Author Charu.

Pratilipi - Princess of heart 'Charu'.

Instagram I'D -Author_Charu2000.

Words shape our world, a tale to share,
Each letter a step, dreams live there.
Names hold our joys, our fears, our might,
Actions push us through day and night.
Colors show feelings, deep in our core,
Bright hopes, dark doubts, the heart's own lore.
How we move forward, quick or slow pace,
Guides our path, lights up the space.
Rules tame the chaos, give meaning a form,
Sentences stand through calm or storm.
Pauses let thoughts find room to grow,
A comma for breath, a dot to show.
Listen to stories, in verse or plain speech,
Each line a lesson, each word a reach.
Speak your truth loud, let your voice sing,
Words change the world with the power they bring.
From ABC's start to wisdom's high aim,
English shows truth in life's great game.
Life's the sentence we write, come what may,
Choose simple words , they show the way.

- *Charu.*

# Co-author Debjani Padhi

Debjani Padhi is born and raised in the temple city, Bhubaneswar, Odisha. She is a teacher by profession. She has a strong aesthetic sense and believes in God in all the stages of her life. She loves to pen her feelings in words. Her writing depicts a true story of emotions.

# Loneliness

My love left me alone,
For a bit of misunderstanding.
I sit up and look around the room in fear,
Sad and engulfed in tears.

My disappointed and distressed heart,
Listens to every beat of explanation,

And understands the steps of miscommunication.

To share my feelings, I chose a place,

Where heaven touches the river,
The leaves rustle and birds chirp,
My fate continues with a coffee sip.

I Hope Bluewater will care for me,
The trees will love and sing for me.
I am quiet as we are part,
We'll try to compromise for a new start.

- *Debjani Padhi.*

# My Princess

My princess, my reality,
You see the truth, in sincerity.
No secrets hide from your sight,
In faith and trust, you shine so bright.

Your world is aligned, with purpose true,
Abiding by lessons, old and new.
With confidence and commitment strong,
You conquer challenges, all day long.

Let go of ego, and self-doubt's sway,
And reflect your inner light of day.
My beloved princess, you bless my life,
Forever shine, with love and strife.

- *Debjani Padhi.*

# Co-author
# Disha Choudhary

Disha Choudhary is a resident of Delhi who loves writing poetries and heartfelt reflections. She finds joy in expressing emotions through words. This is her small attempt to share a piece of her heart with the world.

# A gentle reminder to yourself

Live a little too much.
Smile a little more.
Cry a little less, glow a little more.
Let insecurities go, trust God's plans.
Let people do whatever they want -
You make your inner child happy.
Let life break you, and then heal you.
That's how you learn and grow.
People come and go,
You're the only one who stays with yourself.
Don't let the world be too hard on you.
Be the main character of your life.
Live the way you want.
Spread love and happiness.
Love yourself the way you are.
Life is waiting for you -
Waiting to see you shine.
Don’t let anything ruin you.
You deserve the best.

- *Disha Choudhary.*

# For the tough days

Life always doesn't go the way you want
Sometimes it snatches away everything
From you just to teach you why it's
Important to let go of those things
that don't matter anymore but with a smile
When life doesn't go according to your plans
It doesn't mean this is the end of the story
Maybe it's just a new beginning with some
New people, new experiences, new opportunities, you're
a warrior, who is stronger than you know, greater than
you think, a genuine soul who is going to chase their
dream with hard work & dedication don't let your tough
days be your weakness let them be a reason to go more
harder, be more hardworking but don't let yourself drain
away in this process choose your peace over everything
Maybe that's how we learn to deal with tough times.

- *Disha Choudhary.*

# Co-author
# Disha Shah

Disha Shah – Writer & Changemaker. Disha Shah is a passionate writer and dedicated changemaker whose literary journey began in 2017 with Literary Live. What started as a hobby soon evolved into a meaningful and purposeful pursuit. Over the years, she has actively participated in numerous writing competitions on platforms such as Story Mirror, Mugafi, and others. While she values the excitement of competition, Disha's true aspiration lies in embracing writing as a profession and harnessing its power to drive positive societal change. Her writing seeks to shift perspectives, encourage empathy, and introduce readers to new ideologies. For Disha, writing is more than just a creative outlet—it is a transformative tool to inspire action and deepen understanding. Through her stories and articles, she motivates readers to reflect, grow, and view the world with greater purpose. Disha has contributed to several anthology projects and taken part in many online contests. Her experience as a freelance content writer has further sharpened her adaptability, allowing her to tailor her voice and style to diverse audiences and topics. Firmly believing in the impact of every word, Disha remains committed to crafting narratives that resonate on a personal level. Her work aims to inspire others to chase their dreams, stay true to their values, and help build a more compassionate and thoughtful world.

# Emotions of life

In our lives, we go through many situations that deeply affect our emotions.
Sometimes, we feel completely broken and fed up.
Other times, we feel charged up and full of energy.

These emotional changes happen naturally - they're part of life.

Life is short, and throughout it, we experience a wide range of emotions.
Sometimes, we try and fail again and again. But eventually, we understand that it's all part of the process.

Don't give up.
Instead, accept yourself.
Forgive yourself.

Many times, we're filled with doubt.
But when we start to truly understand ourselves, our lives begin to transform.

We experience anger, sadness, happiness, and more - because emotions are a normal part of being human.

So, never underestimate yourself.
Without emotions, we wouldn't be able to build strong, meaningful relationships.

Emotions are not a weakness — they are what make us human.

- *Disha Shah.*

# Loving yourself, changing everything

Our lives are truly incomplete without emotions.

As human beings, it's in our nature to express what we feel.
But when we express gratitude,
When we show politeness,
When we are loyal,
When we act with compassion -
We connect more easily and deeply with others.

And here's the biggest secret I want to share with you:
The moment you start to love yourself, everything begins to change.

When you begin to truly appreciate and value who you are,
Your life transforms.

People will naturally be drawn to you -
Because when you love yourself, the world feels it.

- *Disha Shah.*

# Co-author

## Dr. Major Nalini Janardhanan

Dr.Major Nalini Janardhanan is a doctor who served in Army, a writer and Akashvani approved artist of Ghazals and Bhajans. She is honored with many awards for her contributions in various fields.

# Happy life

Life is all about happiness and sadness existing together like sunlight and shadow or day and night. On a lighter note, one of my friends recently remarked "Wow…you are like a celebrity woman now! So many awards and achievements... You are living a perfect life!" Seeing the best aspects of other's lives especially on social media, people tend to assume like this. But this is our biggest misunderstanding about others. My friend or others who think like her, never realize the fact that I have my own share of ups and downs in life. They never know about the struggles, disappointments or failures I had in my path of life, ultimately reaching the present position of an achiever with God's blessings. So don't believe that a perfect life means happiness. Your life may not be a fairy tale with 'Then they lived happily ever after' type of ending. It is a mixture of positive and negative events. When you are depressed, believe that 'Nothing lasts forever, this too shall pass'. Stop chasing happiness like a mirage in desert. Learn to accept life as it is. Love yourself. Love your family and friends. Be optimistic with a positive outlook towards life. Love your life! BE HAPPY!

- *Dr Major Nalini Janardhanan.*

# Co-author

## Dr. Richa Biswal

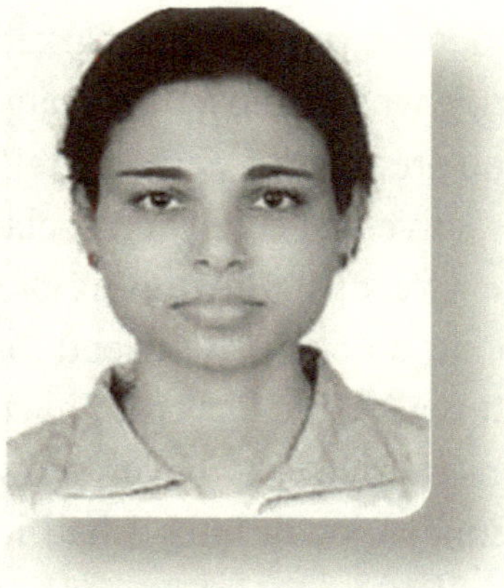

Dr. Richa Biswal is an Assistant Professor in the P.G. Department of English at Maharaja Purna Chandra Autonomous College, Mayurbhanj, Odisha. Her areas of interest include Indian poetics, comparative literature, and aesthetics. She has published several research articles and book chapters in reputed volumes. Passionate about teaching and research, she actively engages in interdisciplinary academic pursuits.

# The margins we leave behind

Each chapter begins with hope in ink,
On paper hearts that softly think.
A cradle laugh, a teardrop's fall,
A rising sun, a midnight call.

The page of joy is gold and bright,
It sings of dreams that chase the light.
Then sorrow comes with silent tread,
And stains the leaves where love had bled.

There's anger sharp, like burning thread,
And envy green, with things unsaid.
But then a page of calm appears—
Forgiveness stitched through folded years.

Desire, like wind, turns every page,
From youthful thirst to wisdom's age.
And courage—quiet, never loud—
Writes in ink both firm and proud.

Some pages blur, some stand apart,
Some end before they even start.
Yet in the spine of every part,
The beating thread—our human heart.

We are the stories we survive,
The bruised, the blooming, still alive.
And every line we've yet to write,
Will glow beneath our fragile light.

So hold your chapter with both hands—
Each word is where a soul still stands.
For in this book of loss and grace,
Every emotion finds its place.

- *Dr. Richa Biswal.*

# The bench by the rain tree

The rain had just stopped. A few lazy droplets clung to the leaves of the old rain tree that stood by the edge of the park, its thick branches stretching like arms frozen mid-embrace. On a worn-out wooden bench beneath it, sat an old man, humming a half-forgotten tune, and a young woman with tear-streaked cheeks.

They hadn't spoken. Not a word.

Mira had come to the park hoping to be alone. Her engagement had just broken—called off over a misunderstanding neither she nor Aarav had the strength to mend. Her eyes were red, her chest heavy with unspoken words. The bench was supposed to be empty, but the old man was already there. Still, something about his presence felt... quiet, kind.

The man looked straight ahead. His eyes weren't focused on anything in particular, yet they seemed full of stories.

After a while, he said, "The tree remembers more love stories than the people sitting beneath it."

Mira turned, startled. He didn't look at her. Just smiled at the horizon.

"I used to bring my wife here," he said. "Same bench. She used to eat mango slices with red chili powder. I never liked the taste, but I ate it anyway because it made her laugh."

Mira smiled weakly.

"Sometimes," he continued, "I think emotions are like seasons. They come uninvited. Stay too long. Leave when you begin to understand them."

Mira finally spoke. "So what do we do when they hurt?"

"Let them," he said gently. "Let them teach you what joy cannot."

Silence again. A leaf fell between them.

After a while, Mira stood up, her heart still bruised but strangely lighter.

"Thank you," she said.

The old man didn't reply. He simply nodded, still smiling.

Mira walked away slowly, the weight on her chest giving way to the rhythm of her footsteps. She didn't know who he was or why he was there, but something about that brief encounter had changed the way her sadness felt—less like drowning, more like learning to breathe underwater.

The old man remained on the bench, humming softly. Another chapter had begun beneath the rain tree.

- *Dr. Richa Biswal.*

# Co-author
# Dr. Rutam Biswal

Dr. Rutam Biswal is a passionate scholar, researcher, and writer. Her academic journey has been marked by consistent excellence—beginning with top ranks in CBSE board exams and culminating in prestigious national fellowships like the DST-INSPIRE (JRF & SRF), CSIR-NET (Rank 29), and GATE. Her research explores innovative materials and their applications, blending modern science with a keen interest in India's traditional knowledge systems. Beyond the laboratory, Dr. Biswal has carved a niche in creative and academic writing. She has won over 30 awards in national and institutional essay contests, including multiple first prizes in the Competition Success Review (CSR) essay series, and the First Prize in the National Research Paper Writing Competition - Vision for Viksit Bharat (2024). Her work reflects a deep commitment to bridging science, culture, and literature. With a drive for discovery and a love for language, she continues to contribute meaningfully to both scientific and literary communities.

# Pages from the book of life

This world is full of tears and fears,
You'll rarely find those joyful cheers.
Problems and struggles crowd your way,
While solutions seem so far away.

You'll find that life's a shifting stage,
With no set script on any page.
To live each moment with a smile is great,
But true joy often makes you wait.

Have faith in that almighty God,
You may also call Him Lord.
Especially for students who face the board,
Or those who can't pay fees they can't afford.

Love, affection, and praise you may get,
But don't get trapped in an unfair net.
For the water-carrier, life stays wet,
For the gambler, life is a risky bet.

Life shows many changing faces,
It shifts its tone in different cases.
Sometimes it's sad, sometimes content -
Moments of peace, then discontent.

Life is like loose grains of sand,
Yet it can turn into a magic wand.
Too much of anything leads to strife,
Where reason drowns in a maddened life.

You'll find sorrow in every hand,
Yet hope still blooms in this vast land.
Life is like deep quicksand -
You slip, you rise, you learn to stand.

- *Dr. Rutam Biswal.*

# **This is life**

When things don't go right
When there is no ray of light,
When there's no place to hide,
And it's too hard to survive,
Tell yourself to go on! This is life.

When there's no friend
When life is on a dead end
When world is not a paradise
When your confidence dies
Tell yourself to go on! This is life.

When there is competition to face
When you are lagging behind in the race.
When you have lost faith in God,
When you are betrayed by a fraud
Tell yourself to go on! This is life.

When your destination is miles apart
When you don't know where to start,
When all you see around is pain,
When your hard work is in vain,
Tell yourself to go on! This is life.

When lessons come wrapped in pain,
When efforts seem to go in vain,

When silence shouts louder than cries,
And truth gets buried under lies,
Tell yourself to go on! This is life.

But when the dawn breaks after the night,
And dreams once lost return to sight,
When strength awakens deep inside,
And hope walks gently by your side -
Smile and whisper with grateful pride: This is life.

- *Dr. Rutam Biswal.*

# Co-author
# Dr. Satwik Chatterjee

Dr. Satwik Chatterjee is a dedicated professional with a strong background in dentistry, psychology, research, and forensic sciences. His academic credentials include a Bachelor's in Dentistry, Fellowship in Forensic Odontology, and Fellowship in Forensic Neuropsychology. He has also pursued postgraduate diplomas in Crime Scene Investigation & Crime Mapping, Forensic Medicine, Toxicology & Medicolegal Autopsy, and Cyber Law & Human Rights Justice. Currently, Dr. Chatterjee is pursuing dual master's degrees in Psychology and Forensic Science, along with a PG Diploma in Psychological Counselling. As a consultant Junior Resident at Appollo Hospital, West Bengal, Dr. Chatterjee is committed to applying his knowledge and skills in real-world settings. He is proud to be a member of several prestigious organizations, including:

1. British Psychological Society
2. Indian Dental Association

3. American Psychological Association
4. World Society of Victimology
5. South Asian Society of Criminology & Victimology
6. American Society of Clinical Oncology
7. Indian Association of Forensic Odontology
8. Tech Forensic Investigation & Global Research
9. Digital Dentistry Society
10. World Leisure Organization

Dr. Chatterjee's research experience spans 53 different projects, and he has been recognized with 4 patents so far (3 Indian and 1 UK). He has worked with esteemed institutions like IISc Bangalore, AIIMS Jodhpur, IIT Kharagpur, ICMR-STS, and NFSU Gandhinagar. Notably, Dr. Chatterjee has received the 'Chancellor's Award, 2025' from Geetanjali University, Udaipur.

# The symphony of our hearts

In the quiet of our hearts, emotions come alive,
A swirling dance of feelings where our spirits thrive.
Joy bubbles up like sunlight, a warmth that makes us glow,
A fleeting burst of laughter where our brightest hopes flow.
It sparks within our minds, a fleeting, tender high,
A moment of pure wonder beneath life's endless sky.

Sorrow slips in softly, a weight we can't ignore,
A quiet ache that lingers, tapping at the core.
It carves a path through memory, both heavy and profound,
Yet in its tender lessons, strength and growth are found.
For grief, though it may wound us, holds a gentle art,
It teaches us to heal and binds the broken heart.

Fear, our wary guardian, with eyes that dart and roam,
Whispers of the shadows where our doubts may call home.
It quickens breath and pulses, a spark to keep us safe,
Yet fuels the fire of courage when we face the fears we chase.
A friend, though often heavy, it nudges us to grow,
To step into the unknown where our braver selves show.

Anger burns like wildfire, a storm within the chest,
A cry for what's been broken, a heart that seeks redress.
It rises fierce and sudden, a spark to right the wrong,
But cooled with understanding, it can make us strong.
It's fuel for change, for justice, when we guide its heated flame,
A force to mend the world or reclaim our rightful name.

Love, oh wild and wondrous, a tide that pulls us near,
A warmth that wraps around us, through joy and pain and fear.
It ties us to each other, a bond that holds us tight,
A messy, perfect magic that lights the darkest night.
It lifts us, breaks us, mends us, in its ever-spinning dance,
The heartbeat of our story, the soul's eternal chance.

And peace, a gentle whisper, when the world grows soft and still,
A moment where the heart rests, where the mind can simply feel.
In quiet, we uncover the truth of who we are,
A canvas of emotions beneath life's guiding star.
Each feeling paints our journey, with colors bold and true,
The hues of all we are, in the life we're passing through.

- *Dr. Satwik Chatterjee.*

## The silent anthem of shattered stars

Sometimes life hums like a melody, tender, full of grace,
Emotions weaving through our days, painting colors on our face.
But there are moments when the song cracks, its notes begin to stray,
When hearts, weighed down by hidden wounds, choose to slip away.

Joy can burst like summer's dawn, a laugh that lights the air,
A fleeting spark where dreams take wing, and hope feels everywhere.
Yet in its glow, a shadow creeps, a quiet ache takes hold,
A hurt that lingers in the soul, unspoken, sharp, and cold.

Sadness falls like endless rain, too heavy for the heart,
Each drop a pang of grief that tears the spirit's core apart.
It settles deep, a silent storm, clouding all we see,
A tide that drowns the light of day, a cage where none are free.

Fear tiptoes in with icy breath, a shiver through the soul,
Whispering of broken paths, of dreams that lose their hold.

It binds the heart in frantic chains, steals breath with every beat,
Makes every step a crumbling edge where hope and despair meet.

Anger flares like wildfire, fierce, a blaze within the chest,
A scream of shame and buried pain that grants the heart no rest.
It twists the mind, it clouds the light, it burns through every seam,
Until the soul feels lost in night, adrift in a shattered dream.

Love, so bold, so warm, so true, can fade within the storm,
When doubt and darkness veil its spark, and distance chills its form.
The hands we cherish, hearts we know, seem worlds away in gloom,
And in that haze, a weary soul may wander toward its doom.

In one hushed moment, overwhelmed, a star may fall from sight,
Choosing silence, choosing dark, to end its desperate fight.
A sudden loss, a fractured song, a light that's gone too

soon,
A heart that couldn't find the dawn beneath its heavy moon.

But oh, if we could see the hurt that hides behind the eyes,
Could clasp the hand that trembles, hear the heart's unspoken cries.
Each soul's a fragile constellation, yearning for the light,
A spark that craves a gentle touch to guide it through the night.

So let's reach out, let's hold them close, to every whispered plea,
To lift the ones who falter, to set their spirits free.
For in this life, where joy and pain in tangled chords entwine,
Every soul deserves a hand, a chance to brightly shine.

- *Dr. Satwik Chatterjee.*

# Co-author
# Ishani Ganguly

Ishani Ganguly, a sorceress of syllables and a cartographer of human ache, sculpts poetry not for applause but for alchemy. Her pen, dipped in dusk and desire, resurrects the emotions time tried to bury. With a soul stitched from mythology & marrow marinated into metaphors, Ishani crafts verses that echo like forgotten lullabies through the corridors of existence. Her language is rich, her rhythm ancient- like scrolls unearthed from civilizations that once felt too deeply. She believes poetry is not penned- it is conjured, and each of her lines bears witness to the wars between silence and sentiment. Ishani does not merely write- she remembers, bleeds, and baptizes the page.

# When silence learned to scream

## Sub-title: A Ballad of the Unheard Heart

The dawn was draped in a veil of hush,
Where even winds forgot to rush,
And in that stillness bloomed a cry-
A whisper dressed in lullaby.

She walked on thoughts like shattered
glass,
Each step- a chronicle of the past.
Her shadow stitched from buried scars,
Danced beneath the weeping stars.

The world had books, but not her tale,
Her breath was ink- her lungs, the grail.
The Gods, too deaf for mortal ache,
Slept soundly by the judgement take.

Emotions swam in molten lead,
Her smile- a script the poets dread.
The thunder wore her name in rage,
Yet silence locked her in its cage.

She learned to scream in voiceless art,
To carve her storms in aging heart.
Her tears could chisel granite lore,

Yet no one heard the ocean roar.

A mirror watched her hope erode,
On avenues that grief bestowed.
But when she danced with doom's ballet,
The night, ashamed , turned into day.

A war within, she dared to win,
Her pain- a hymn, her loss- a hymn.
In silence now, her soul may gleam-
For she, at last, taught scream to dream.

- *Ishani Ganguly.*

# The lanthern that bled blue

## Sub-title: An Elegy of Eternal Waiting

I saw a lantern by the shore,
It wept in hues the stars ignore.
A sapphire wick, a crimson sigh,
Flickered beneath a frostbit sky.

Time, the blind minstrel, strummed his lyre,
While fate lit candles made of fire.
And in that glow, a story stood-
A tale too grave for brotherhood.

She waited- not for man or beast,
But for a promise long deceased.
His voice still echoed in her chest,
Like moonlight trapped in raven's nest.

Her eyes, two mausoleums bright,
Where ghosts of smiles kissed sleepless night.
Her breath smelled like unfinished verse,
Her veins- a map the Gods would curse.

She fed the flame with ancient grief,
Each wick a wound beyond belief.

Her hands, embalmed in yearning's
thread,
Stitched lullabies for what was dead.

The tides would kneel to her despair,
As though the sea could learn to care.
Even the stars grew pale with guilt,
Watching her world, heartbreak-built.

Yet she would wait- till lanterns bled,
Till all the oaths her lover said.

- *Ishani Ganguly.*

# Co-author
# Kajal Sahu

Kajal Sahu is a passionate writer and a postgraduate student of Psychology. Daughter of Mr. Kishore Sahu and Mrs. Champa Sahu, she has contributed as a co-author in more than 30 published books, showcasing her love for writing and creative expression

# When the pen held my hand

When the world around me quietly broke,
And not a single soul heard the words I never spoke
I sat in silence, heavy with pain,
Until the pen whispered, "Let it pour like rain."

The page opened its arms without a sound,
And in that moment, a part of me was found.
Every line I wrote carried my scars,
Yet turned my darkness into stars.

Poetry didn't ask questions or judge my fall,
It simply listened and healed it all.
And that's how I learned, in the silence so deep,
Some chapters of life don't hurt they help us breathe.

- *Kajal Sahu.*

# Just a chapter of life

You were a part of my story, not the whole book,
Just a small turn, not the path I took.
I felt love, and yes, I felt pain,
Waited for you but you never came.

You were not there when I was low,
Still, I smiled and let you go.
No anger in heart, no need to cry,
Some goodbyes happen without a "why."

You were a chapter, short and fast,
But life goes on the pain won't last.
Now I'm moving on, calm and free,
Because the best part of life, is still waiting for me.

- *Kajal Sahu.*

# **Co-author**
# **Karan Dhingra**

Karan Dhingra, a 16-year-old, living in Delhi. He is someone who loves to write, read, speak. He feels literature. He hopes to be an established writer, someday he will be other than that. He loves biology and science, to cook, paint, design, do debates. He is everything but a teenager.

# Validate me?

If I make a hole in time and space, in your heart, in our relationship, can you still validate me, love me unconditionally, so beautifully that even nature weeps tears of envy, will you let me keep my head on your chest, let me listen to my mistakes, if I end all of this know, can you tell me please, that I was right all along, I wasn't cursed, after all our story isn't a fable, if I punch the wall, and envelope a hole, will you tell me anger is a weird thing, will you validate me love, will the souvenirs I get you always stay on your fridge's door, even if I say I don't like you anymore, will you let me curse you when I know I am wrong, but I don't want to bow down, if I tell you earth is shaped like a diamond, will you tell me I am right, will you be the wool ball I will be the mice, only if you keep validating me, it will get hard, you will think to pull me apart, tear the photographs, But will you still validate me, validate me?

- *Karan Dhingra.*

# I don't

I don't love and tell, I don't love and forget, what even is love if not sulking in it, the thought of you never marooned me, if cupids are a myth, then who hit me, if our paths our intertwined why hadn't you kissed me, I only love this, feeling hopelessly romantic, curiously frantic to lose this feeling, to forget this reeling, nothing is about me, when you stand there in the restaurants dim light, asking them waiter about the drinks, speaking so softly, that the air passes my cheeks, how bad I want to grace those cheeks, that mauve hue, those coffee stained lips, why wouldn't anyone love this, why couldn't I confess this, maybe because I don't want to be unsatisfied with the reality, because my delusions might be too beating, or maybe my love language is that of secrecy, after all, I have always loved you in secrecy, you are too pretty to be with me, but I can't forget to love you so easily, so early.

- *Karan Dhingra.*

# Co-author
# Kirti Verma

Kirti is from Kanpur, she is author, poet & student (pursuing journalism from Bhopal). She compiled 5 anthologies! She also worked in so many publications and writing communities & she loves to perform poetry in open mics & also review the books! You can connect with her through Instagram - @thekirtiverma. & @books_with_kirti.

# Father

He was someone who can make me happy, who can handle all my moods, who can handle my craziness, who can handle me at every situation, who can make me feel comfortable in every place. The only person I can listen to silently is my father. He was the one who told me how to say no without disrespecting anyone. He was someone who is always with me, no matter what the situation is! He was someone who never listen anyone but he listened mine! He was the only person who can handle my everything! When he was there, I never get afraid of anyone! He was someone who can lightens my whole day! He was the only person who can tease me whole day & I never get irrigated! I hope you are watching me dadda!

- *Kirti Verma.*

# Co-author Mayank Kumar

Just a writer

# Grateful for your presence

Phrases written on you
With gratitude, love and care
A Poem meant for you
For everything you share

You are a star in my darkest night
You will always be my guiding light
I would take a moment to Thank You
For always being so true

There are memories we share
You are someone so rare
I am grateful for your presence
And for being there to defense

Supportive, loyal and so kind
A friend like you so rare to find
For every memory we shared
Thank you, my friend, for always being there

- *Mayank.*

# Co-author

## Mr. Saroj Kumar Ojha

Teacher, Poet and writer, Mr. Saroj Kumar Ojha, a well-known name and a well-known exemplary teacher. Odisha Elementary Education system is appreciated from various quarters as an efficient worker who wishes a bright future for the students by entering the education system. As a well-known face, his written words have spread around the world and taken him to the top. He has also come to the society as an environmentalist who believes in the environment and has a healthy mentality of environmental protection. As proof, he has glorified the region by receiving PRAKRUTIBANDHU Award from Odisha Environment, Forest and Climate Change Department, Bhubaneswar. Recently, his Two English books of Articles, Edu Light and Unique feeling have been published. So, Mr. Ojha is such a unique good man which is unimaginable.

# Severe emotional life

Feelings are my passion.
Life goes on and on.
I smile and laugh at everyone.
I give my word as long as I live.
How many times will the hopes of the heart come true?
Everyone is a deceiver in this world.
They release poison in words.
They hide anger in their eyes with gestures.
They show devotion on the surface,
But it is not seen otherwise inside.
In a world of lies,
There is no truth in words,
They do not have the patience to speak.
Why do people take birth?
There are four hundred words in every word,
The poison is filled in every heart,
The feeling of hatred is not known.
In that, people show light,
Or at least a truthful person,
Everyone knows his nature.
One day or another,
If they lose faith,
They will die.
No one will approach them in such a way,
No one will even talk,
They will take their own lives.

Woe to them,
How they are living their lives.
Whoever poisons their faith.
They are the soul killers of this nation.
Honesty is not a virtue,
Why is it so?
Tell me, who knows.
Once in a lifetime,
Benefit others.
There is no writing in the birth certificate.
What kind of work will you do in life,
God knows everything.
If there is nothing true in a thousand verses,
A curse will surely fall.
Be proud of an evil friend.
You will definitely get punished,
Know that.
If you do not become aware now,
You will surely fall into hell and die.
See the good as a remembrance of love.
Life will be blessed.

- *Saroj Kumar Ojha.*

# Co-author
# Pradnya – Athreya Narawade

Pradnya-Athreya Narawade is a young Indian writer whose words walk the delicate line between poetry and lived truth. Rooted in emotional honesty, her writing explores themes of self-discovery, vulnerability, and inner strength. She believes emotions aren't something to escape - but something to understand, express, and evolve through. Whether it's through metaphor, memoir, or gentle rebellion, her work carries the quiet intensity of someone who feels deeply but never writes for mere performance.

Her unique style - introspective, fluid, and subtly powerful - resonates with anyone who has ever tried to find meaning in chaos or stillness in noise. Pradnya doesn't just write stories; she writes feelings that stay.

When she's not weaving words into verses, she shares her reflections on her blog [streamedwords.wordpress.com] and her Instagram writing page @_wordsthatstaydnya, where her growing community connects with her deeply personal and poetic expressions. In “Chapters of Life”, her contribution “The Unskipped Chapters” invites readers into a journey of emotional reclamation - a reminder that even the quietest voices can echo the loudest truths.

# The unskipped chapters

Some chapters in life come without titles.
They begin like whispers,
then become storms,
before quieting into lessons we didn't ask for.

I've lived those pages.
The ones where everything looked perfect from a distance,
but unraveled thread by thread when held too close.
The ones where smiles didn't mean safety,
and warmth came with conditions.
But emotions have their own language -
they don't need logic to be real.

There was a time I confused closeness with connection.
When silence between words felt louder than words themselves.
But life -
it has a way of revealing truths in pauses,
in things left unsaid,
in the way people show up or don't.

And so I began learning myself in reverse.
Unbecoming the things I was taught to tolerate.
Learning that kindness without boundaries isn't virtue -
it's self-erasure.

That softness isn't weakness,
unless handed to the wrong hands.

But this isn't a story of loss.
This is a story of becoming.
Of feeling deeply without apology,
of growing quietly in spaces where no one thought I would bloom.

I didn't just heal -
I created.
Words became more than an escape.
They became return.
To the girl who used to hide her voice in fear of being too much,
and now spills emotions like poetry with a spine of steel.

Some days, I write to remember.
Others, to release.
But always with the truth of emotion -
not curated for comfort,
but raw,
honest,
alive.

And then there came a softness.
A presence - not loud,
not grand -

but steady.
The kind that doesn't ask you to change
but reminds you you're already enough.
That not all silence is emptiness -
some of it is peace.

That's the beauty of emotions -
they evolve.
They don't stay in heartbreak forever.
They shift.
They teach you to feel again,
this time with both eyes open
and your heart no longer begging,
just being.

I've stopped rushing to the happy ending.
I'm learning to sit in the middle -
where the mess is,
where the doubt lives,
where becoming happens.

Because we aren't meant to be perfect.
We're meant to be real.
We are made of breath, and pauses, and sudden laughter,
and quiet sobs that no one sees.
We carry storms in our ribcage
and still wake up to chase light.

So, if you're reading this
and you've ever felt too emotional,
too sensitive,
too open,
just know -
you are exactly enough.
Because to feel
is to live fully.
To break and build and bloom again.

My name is Pradnya Narawade,
and I'm still writing -
through the ache,
through the calm,
through every chapter that dared to change me.

This isn't the end.
It's a page turned,
a breath taken,
a life felt deeply -
and lived without skipping a single emotion.

- *Pradnya-Athreya Narawade.*

# Beyond the window

There's a kind of presence that fills the room,
without ever speaking.
A silence that becomes furniture -
always there,
never touched.

Some bonds aren't loud.
They don't arrive with confessions
or goodnight texts.
They exist quietly -
in half-open doors,
unfinished sentences,
and the steady sound of someone breathing
on the other side of the wall.

I grew up around such stillness.
It wasn't cold -
just distant.
Not unkind -
just unreadable.
And yet,
it taught me how to sit with myself.
To find poetry in routine,
and love in unspoken rituals.

There was always a window.

The kind that didn't swing wide open
but let enough light in
to remind you that the world is still there,
even if it feels far.

From that window,
I watched shadows stretch and shorten with time.
I watched someone walk in and out of days
without ever really arriving.
There was a rhythm to it -
like footsteps memorized by the floor.
Consistent. Predictable. Distant.

Not once did I ask for closeness.
Not because I didn't need it,
but because I knew
some people speak in actions,
not words.
Some love you best
from the other side of the glass.

And so I learned to read gestures.
How a warm plate left behind
can feel like an apology.
How a shared umbrella
can replace a thousand unsaid things.
How care can sit in silence
and still echo.

But even now,
in the quiet hours,
there are questions I tuck away
like unsent letters.
Did they ever want to say more?
Did they ever wait for me
to open the window first?

Some connections don't break.
They just stretch across time
like thin threads -
never snapping,
never quite pulling close.
And maybe that's enough.
Maybe love doesn't always have to be loud
to be real.

Sometimes,
it's just the act of staying.
Even if it's from a distance.
Even if it's
from beyond the window.

- *Pradnya-Athreya Narawade.*

# Co-author

## Pranali Vijay Patil

It's Pranali Patil & her hobbies is reading books & writing articles & many more. And, also the good painting.

# Everything is temporary

The one thing that will change your life forever is accepting that everything is temporary. Happiness. Pain. Failure. Success. Your relationships. Your entire existence is temporary and the fact that you can't be sure whether you will live another day is enough to show you that whatever it is you're stressing about -it will pass. Happiness and pain are both fleeting, sprinkled throughout the larger chapters that make up our entire lives. Lives that can pass with a blink of an eye. So, what's the point of comparison? Of wanting what other people have and feeling like a failure if you don't get it? What is the point of holding grudges and letting your ego direct your behaviour, and letting your mind take hold of your relationships in a way that your heart wouldn't? Knowing that this exact moment will never come back should be enough to urge you to pick up the phone and make that call. It should be enough to make you realise that if you're in a difficult place right now hurting, frustrated, upset over something that you don't have any control over -give yourself time. You won't be here forever. Neither in pain, nor in happiness. So, make the most of it. Forgive more easily, learn to push away the bad stuff, and accept growth in ways that benefit not just you but everyone around you. Let go of all the negative feelings and animosity and be kind. Be soft. Be gentle with other people. And remind yourself that if today was painful, if today was awful, if today was nothing like what you had hoped it would be tomorrow will be better. Tomorrow will be better.

- *Pranali Vijay Patil.*

# When life feels heavy

At some point in life, everything around you might stop making sense. The job you once prayed for no longer excites you. The home you used to find comfort in starts to feel heavy. You'll feel disconnected from your purpose, unsure about your business, distant from your family, tired of trying to hold it all together. It'll feel like everything is breaking at the same time. And in that weight, you'll feel this aching need to fix yourself, to fix your life, to go back to the starting point and question if you even chose the right direction. Maybe you're already there. Maybe you're standing in the middle of the chaos right now, watching your relationships shake, your finances shrink, your health shift,and wondering if any of it still makes sense.

If that's where you are, I want you to pause. Just for a second. And remember how far you've already come. You've carried yourself through more than you give yourself credit for. You've survived days you thought would break you. You'll be okay. As always.

- *Pranali Vijay Patil.*

# Co-author

# Jayaprakash

Jayaprakash, B.com is working in Chennai international Airport as Document controller and junior accountant.

We used to talk with eyes alone,
Now silence fills the space we've grown.
Your laughter lingers in the air,
But when I reach, there's nothing there.

A thousand words I never said,
Now echo loud inside my head.
I miss the quiet that we shared -
The kind that said you truly cared.

So here I sit in quiet pain,
Wishing I could hold you again.

- *Jayaprakash.*

# Co-author
# Rangeesh Chandrasekar

Rangeesh Chandrasekar is an MBA Finance and Marketing graduate staying in Chennai, Tamilnadu. He is passionate about writing and a great lover of books and articles who has Co Authored and Compiled several anthologies now.

# Men have pains too

A woman said to me, "It took me years to really know that men cry too. I took my husband for a super human. I see him leave the house every day and come back providing for us. One day as I have left the house and he was at home, I remembered that I needed to take something along, I turned back and headed home. As I got home, I tried going through the back door which was closer the window of our room. Heard my husband crying like baby asking God to help me get a job so I can help him to defend for the family. He has never complained to me before but that day, I broke down in tears realizing, my husband has held much of his pains alone."

A young married lady went to her mother and believe that her husband has not always bought things she wanted from him. The mother asked her, "How man those things have you bought for yourself?". She stayed quiet and said, "But he is my husband?". The mother replied her, "Have you ever found out the things your husband wants you to buy for him?".

Men always try to hide their pains. Men can be financially broke and pretend to have everything. Most men are married but they have lonely life. Sometimes, ask your husband out. Men are not always busy as women think. You have to understand that your husband has pains and needs too. Don't judge him by things you want from him. Sometimes, your husband doesn't have things you want. Men also have emotional needs and problems. Men still cry for love.

- *Rangeesh Chandrasekar.*

# Co-author
# Reem Sayed

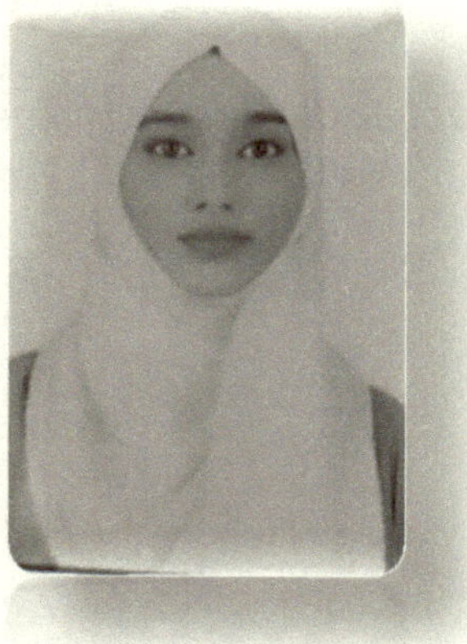

A Graduate pursuing her master's in Business Administration (MBA) at Poona Institute of Managerial and Entrepreneurial sciences Affiliated to the SPPU. Reading and poetry comes naturally to all those who want to be touched by the magic of philosophy, literature and music. Life often makes one a lyricist at heart, making it bearable to unravel the various enigmas of daily mundanity. Food and literature always tend to revive the essence of life, making the notion of existence a bit enthralling and the whole affair worthwhile.

# Life, renewal or revival?

Laying lifelessly on a withering leaf,
In a tiny cranny, One could catch a glimpse,
Fidgeting within, was a pupa, greatly fragile, undergoing a transformation, rather not brief,
Enormous droplets cloud my vision as I peer closely,
A trip down memory lane, when little me wondered that caterpillars perished to transfigure into a Butterfly,
Just as the intensity of the rain escalated sharply, a tiny squirrel scurried off,
Orangish hues were the leaves bespeckled with, threatening an early autumn,
Under the sprawling shade of the golden Oak, I silently stood,
Relishing and reviving in the magic of nature, unfurling leisurely multi-dimensional,
New York City had never seemed so picturesque ever, with droplets reflecting rainbows, while clinging onto a leaf's periphery,
Embracing the soothing breeze, I contemplated, how one life leads onto another, is this what life equates to, a cycle perpetual (or metamorphically?)
Yestereve, it may feel like, as I sensed time pause for what seemed like an eternity.

- *Reem Sayed.*

# Co-author

## Santhosh Kumar RJ

Santhosh Kumar R.J, born on June 11, 1974, is a multifaceted educator, writer, and motivator, served as the Executive Officer and Principal of a higher secondary school. He holds a rich educational background with degrees in English, Hindi, Journalism, and Education Management. Fluent in multiple languages, including Tamil, English, Hindi, Sanskrit, French and Malayalam with German. Santhosh is a prolific author, having written over 150 school-oriented books and several trilingual dictionaries. His literary contributions include translations of Thirumandhiram and Thirukural into Hindi, alongside original works such as "Meeti Yaden, Manuaa, Man ko banao Mahaan, Man-Smrithi collection of Hindi poems. LALL. a collection of english poems. He has penned over 2,500 poems, thousands of stories, dramas, and essays, with numerous translations of literary works between Tamil and Hindi. Santhosh's writings have been published in various prestigious magazines and newspapers across India.

Recognized for his literary and educational impact, he has received numerous awards, including the Sahitya Samrat and Dr. B.R. Ambedkar Talent Research National Award. His work has garnered appreciation from prominent figures, including a few Chief Ministers and the secretary of Indian Prime Minister Narendra Modi.

# Embrace the effective

Fear not, fear not ever, as fear kills your motion
There are evidences of incidents that fear kills the action
The fear of failure stops you to think and act
The fear of being alone makes you sacrifice

The fear of family burden keeps one unmarried
The fear of sickness makes you avoid so many things
Keep smiling, let your face glow without makeup
Keep smiling, let your smile light up the faces that see you

Keep smiling, as it is the key to having more relations
Keep smiling, this is the only adorable emotion of life
Laugh loudly, let others join you without condition
Never laugh at others' actions, it will hurt people

All noble people of the world are aware that anger is danger
Your anger hurts others, makes them feel sad
Are you aware that your anger hurts you and your body?
Anger kills your inner self, hurts you and the listener

Anger keeps everyone at a distance from you forever
Anger is danger; find a way to manage it
There are sweet gestures and lots more of sweet words
Use the sweetest words that make the listener and

yourself happy

Kind words will make your heart kind and bring light
Use the sweetest words, and you will be of your own kind
Bitter words worsen the environment and efforts
Be kind, be the sweetest person who is loved by all

Gossiping may be pleasurable for a few
You make it a habit to fulfill the evil-natured self-satisfaction
Few girls and so many women keep some taps in their eyes
With reason, sometimes without reason, we open the taps

Tears flow with utmost force as they open the taps
Melting the hearts of good ones viewing this scene
Never cry in front of others to showcase your emotions
Never ever lose heart; this will bring all problems

Love is the most powerful and enjoyable feeling
Let's spread love and be lovely in every walk of life
Love all, live for everyone; your life will be worthy
Spread love and peace; the world will turn to heaven

Life is not certain; it has an end today or in future
Lead the life which shall be remembered by all

Troublesome is hated by all throughout the world
Peacemaker is remembered by everyone every time

Life is a gift of God; let us gift love to all who live with us
Let love pave the way and make life lovable
Let our emotions make the life of people happy
Live like legends who used love as the only weapon.

- *Santhosh Kumar.R.J*

# Shivangi Jaiswal

# Co-author
# Shivangi Jaiswal

Shivangi Jaiswal is a versatile writer, compiler of over 60 anthologies, and co-author in 200+ published works. She has been honoured by the Indian Book of Records and Bravo International Book of Records for her literary achievements. Her writing often explores themes of emotion, healing, identity, and quiet strength.With a style that blends poetry and introspection, she gives voice to the silences many carry within.For Shivangi, writing isn't just art - it's therapy, rebellion, and a way of breathing. She believes that the most powerful stories are the ones that feel like truth.

# Emotions of life: The colors we never learn to name

There are moments in life that don't make noise when they arrive.
Like the evening your friend walks away without saying goodbye.
Or the morning you stare at your coffee a little too long, wondering why it doesn't taste the same anymore.

These aren't headline emotions.
They don't come with warning signs or grand gestures.
But they stay - quietly, stubbornly - inside your chest, rearranging the way you feel the world.

That's the thing about life:
It doesn't hand you one emotion at a time.
It throws them all at once - joy laced with guilt, love dipped in fear, silence echoing with anger.

We grow up learning nouns: success, love, failure, peace.
But nobody teaches us how to live with the verbs: hurting, healing, hoping, hiding.

- *Shivangi Jaiswal.*

## The beauty in feeling everything

And yet, how beautiful it is to feel.
To hurt deeply means you loved deeply.
To be anxious means you still care about what happens next.
Even numbness - painful as it is - is your mind protecting you from too much feeling at once.

We're taught to be strong,
but not how to feel safely.
We're told not to cry, but not taught how to process grief.
So we build walls, wear masks, laugh at our pain -
and call it "moving on."

But emotions are not flaws.
They're not weakness.
They are proof that you are alive.
That despite the heaviness of living, you still carry the capacity to feel -
and that, in itself, is strength.

- *Shivangi Jaiswal.*

# Co-author

## Shroddha Mukherjee

Shroddha Mukherjee has done graduation from bachelor of fine arts (Applied Art). Completing master's from photography, and she love to write poetry. And developed interest in writing by reading the books of - William Shakespeare, William Blake, William Wordsworth and Robert Frost. She has been writing since 2018. She is the author of 17 + different types of anthologies till now. She is also a published her own book name 'Something Won't Be Changed!' In her view: 'Patience is the key of success when you dream about something then make sure you can't die before converting your dreams into reality because you see your dreams with your younger age it needs more time to bring you your reward. If you've patience, then try hard for your dreams to successful to succeed in life!' Instagram id: @shroddhawrites._

# **I'm thunder rippling in the dark**

You are there to find out your
strengths and find out your flaws,
aren't you?

If you have to take a step forward
then there are people to pull you back...

If you want to dream then
there are people to make
you look high and make you look bad...

You ignite the spark of passion within
yourself, people are there to burn, right?

If you want to love then do it yourself,
there are people to hate...!

You create your own identity
and walk in the crowd, right?

You do something and show the world
that people are there to applaud...!!

I am thunder rippling in the dark
As the raindrops wound
the already fragile hearts..!

Sorrow falling upon the world like a blanket, Wondering
how much longer
our broken souls can take it..!

I am lost when the storm
shatters the world,
Breaking the glass as the space
between the lines unfurl..!
And wandering like no man wanders before, Hanging
from the busted seam brought by greed, hunger, and war,
Never allowing their dreams to wash upon a dusty
shore..!!

P.s.: Deciding to compare that of my mind, soul, and body to an element, I chose lightning..
To have the characteristics of lighting, I feel as if one must be vibrant against a black sky and bursting with passion as lighting does electricity.. All of us are lighting one way or another.. No matter the way one chooses to express their inner lighting, just remember that the small bit of electricity is there and it is alive..~ That's all..!!

- *Shroddha.*

## **Dear life, please forgive me**

No one knew the battle she fought
inside of her everyday..

But no matter how dark it go,
She kept her smile and shined her light
for anyone who needed it..

Even though she knew she was
the one who needed it the most..

She passed hardest moments alone while everyone else
believed
She was fine...!!

Courage becomes less and less day by day
And life also turned from bad to worse,

The call kept calling me
And then who knows when
and where she got lost,

Whenever I returned,
I always collided with the stars..
She kept running away from
everyone and then sat down
somewhere tired of crying;

And today I don't know where
my condition has disappeared..

Narrating my stories
This happened,
my voice has also turned to stone...!!!

- *Shroddha.*

# Co-author
# Shruti Samskruti

Shruti Samskruti is a dedicated student of B.A. (Hons.) Sanskrit from the Faculty of Arts, Banaras Hindu University. She has actively participated in academics and co-curricular activities, earning recognition in essay writing, debates, and research presentations. Her achievements include the first prize in the CSR Junior Essay Contest (2021) and top ranks in national-level competitions like Bharat Ko Jano (2017) and Bhartiya Vaibhav Gyan Pariksha (2024). With a sincere interest in learning and knowledge-sharing, she continues to grow through diverse academic experiences.

# Chapters of life

Life is a book with pages wide,
Where tears and laughter both reside.
Each chapter opens with a start,
A joy, a scar, a beating heart.

Some pages sing of childhood days,
Of careless laughs and sunshine rays.
Then teenage storms come crashing in,
With restless dreams and silent sin.

Love writes its part in velvet ink,
And loss arrives before we blink.
Some chapters glow, some slowly fade,
Some promises are never made.

We turn the page, we grow, we bend,
Not every tale has a clear end.
But every line we've lived and penned
Becomes the soul we learn to send.

So read your life, both dark and bright -
Each word a step toward deeper light.

- *Shruti Samskruti.*

# Lines we live

Life is written in quiet lines,
In whispered hopes and hidden signs.
Each chapter starts with something new,
A face, a fear, a dream come true.

One page may shine with pure delight,
The next may steal your sleep at night.
Some verses sting, some heal the soul,
Some leave you shattered, some feel whole.

We laugh, we break, we fall, we rise,
We search for truth behind the lies.
Old friendships fade, new ones begin,
Some stories lose, some stories win.

Not all the tales are clean or clear,
Some start with doubt, but end sincere.
The ink may blur, the plot may shift -
But every scar becomes a gift.

So read each line, don't skip or race -
Your story moves with quiet grace.

- *Shruti Samskruti.*

# Co-author
# Simran Thapa

Simran Thapa writes stories that touch the heart, especially about love, emotions, and human connections. Through her words, she tries to capture feelings we all go through: Joy, heartbreak, hope, and healing. Writing is her way of understanding the world and sharing it with others.

thapasimran132@gmail.com.

# Mismatched

"Wait - you like this show too?"
That's how it started.
Well, well. Let's start from the beginning.
It was the 13th of December, 2024 - the day Mismatched Season 3 was released. I was so excited because it's one of my all-time favourite shows. After the lecture, I decided to binge-watch it - I just couldn't stop myself.
As I was watching, he noticed and asked, "New season aa gaya?"
I smiled and replied, "Yes!" Then I added, "Tujhe bhi yeh series pasand hai?"
He said yes, and that's how we started talking.
Over the next few days, our conversations revolved around the show. I used to proudly give him spoilers, and he'd groan every time. He even started calling me "Dimple" (the name of the main character) every time he saw me.
And then came February. Our classes had themed events - Bollywood Day, Traditional Day, and more. One day before Bollywood Day, I called him and asked, "Tu kya ban raha hai?"
He laughed and said, "Rooh Baba from Bhool Bhulaiyaa 2."
As soon as I heard that, I said, "No way!"
"Tu kya ban rahi hai?" he asked.
I replied, "Stree from Stree."

We both burst out laughing - it was the perfect Bhoot and Baba duo.
Since we were classmates, he used to tease me about literally anything. And every time the lecture ended, I'd pack up and leave quickly - but somehow, he'd always come down at the same time. I don't know if it was just a coincidence, but we always ended up talking.
Whenever something was going on in my life, I'd tell him—and he would always listen, patiently, giving advice like he genuinely cared.
Days passed like this… and then came my birthday.
He was the first person to wish me - exactly at 12:00 AM.
For the first time, after my family, someone else had celebrated my birthday. He did. And I don't know how to explain it, but I was so happy… and honestly, a little emotional too. It meant more than I thought it would.
After that, we started spending even more time together.
We had a cricket match coming up, and for two whole days, I was there, cheering for him and supporting his team. And they won.
I was so happy - as if I was the one playing on the field.
His victory felt like mine.
That day changed something - I didn't want to miss out on time with him anymore. I started coming to class regularly and staying till 6 PM… just to be around him a little longer.
As the days passed, I didn't even realize how or when it happened - but I started falling for him.

And the strange thing is… I never expected it. It just happened.

It was so easy to be around him, so natural - like I was slowly reconnecting with a version of myself I had forgotten. The feelings were new, unfamiliar. I had never felt this way about someone so soon.

He made it hard not to fall for him - with his cute smile, his warm brown eyes, his voice. Even on my worst days, just seeing his face was enough to make me smile like an idiot.

In such a short time, the bond we shared was something I had never experienced before - with anyone.

But deep down, I knew… he would never fall for me.

He hadn't moved on from his past. And I could see it - it was still there, in the way he talked, the way he looked away when love came up.

It wasn't easy for him. And I understood that.

So, I decided I would never tell him how I felt.

But my eyes… my eyes said it all.

And maybe that's why everyone around us seemed to know.

Because no matter how hard I tried to hide it, anyone could see how much I adored him.

And the truth is… I've never been good at hiding my emotions.

My face says it all.

Even he noticed that.

One day, he looked at me and simply said,

"I know you have feelings for me… but I don't have feelings for you."

I smiled, though it hurt more than I'd ever admit.

"It's okay," I replied softly. "I knew it since day one. We can be best friends."

I meant it. Or at least I tried to.

But then, just a few days later… everything changed.

Out of nowhere, he looked at me and said,

"I think I have feelings for you too."

And just when I thought my heart couldn't take any more surprises, he added,

"But I need some time to think about it."

I nodded, trying to hide the storm of emotions behind my calm smile.

"Take all the time you need," I said softly. And I meant it.

Because feelings, when real, should never be rushed.

And even after that conversation… we never stopped talking.

We were best friends.

Just like before—laughing over inside jokes, sharing random memes, teasing each other during class. Nothing really changed on the outside. But I knew, deep down, something had shifted in me.

I still had feelings for him.

And maybe he was still figuring it out.

But I didn't let it ruin what we had.

Being around him still felt like home - safe, silly, comforting.

He always made sure I was okay - helping me with little things, checking up on me when I didn't even realize I needed it. Whether it was saving a seat for me, waiting till I packed up, or noticing when my mood was off - he just knew.

He protected me, sometimes silently, like walking on the side of the road without being asked, or standing up for me when I wasn't even around to see it.

He took care of me - not in some dramatic way, but in all the soft, invisible ways that only someone who truly pays attention can.

His presence made life feel a little lighter. A little easier.

And every time he looked at me and smiled, it was enough to keep the hope alive, even if just a little.

Who would've thought… that a random series conversation would give me the best bond I've ever had—the best person who walked into my life at just the right time. And even the best thing that's ever happened to me.

We never labeled what we had.

We just kept showing up for each other - in small ways, in quiet moments, in late-night. Maybe we were more than friends. Maybe we weren't.

But even today, we're still best friends…

with feelings tucked quietly between the lines.

And just like that…

My second love story became something unforgettable.

Not perfect. Not planned.

But ours.

And that made it everything. You're my beginning, middle and end.

- *Simran Thapa.*

# Co-author
# Suraj Kumar

Suraj Kumar is a burgeoning writer and creative artist born in Haryana, India. At just 16 years old, he has already begun making a name for himself with his evocative works that traverse the complexities of life. His writing spans multiple mediums, including song lyrics (available on SoundCloud and Audiomack), poetry, and prose, often exploring themes of love, self-discovery, and personal growth. With a distinctive voice and perspective, Suraj seeks to inspire and resonate with readers across generations. As he continues to hone his craft, he remains driven by a passion for storytelling that propels him to push creative boundaries and explore new ideas.

# Origami of the unsaid

I learned to swim in my mother's tears,
each stroke a prayer she couldn't speak.

Words became weapons before I knew
their weight. Sorry never healed
what I carved with my tongue.

Grandmother's hands fold origami birds
from hospital receipts. She teaches me
that everything beautiful
breaks first.

The radio between stations -
that's where I found God,
in the space between certainty
and silence.

Tonight I sit with blank pages,
wondering if some stories
choose their own endings.

When I die, burn my notebooks.
Let the smoke spell out
what I was too afraid
to say alive.

The chapters write themselves -
we just hold the pen
until our fingers cramp
and the story
swallows us whole.

- *Suraj Kumar.*

# Watercolor chapters

We are born mid-sentence -
a comma in someone else's story,
blinking into the soft static of becoming.

Childhood is a prologue with jam-stained fingers,
truth told in crayon,
grief hiding in tree hollows and nightlight prayers.

Then comes the page-turn:
adolescence, all wildfire and mirrors,
fists full of questions no one dares to answer.
You call it chaos,
but it's just the soul trying to fit
inside skin that keeps rewriting its edges.

Adulthood arrives like footnotes -
bills, bruises, routines that flatten
dreams into digestible schedules.
You learn to fold your rage
into polite conversation,
to mourn in motion.

But somewhere -
between a funeral and a first kiss,
a war protest and your grandmother's laugh -
you realize:

life was never linear.

Each chapter bleeds
into the next like watercolor
on cheap paper.

There is no climax,
only crescendos of quiet courage:
choosing to stay,
choosing to change,
choosing to love
after being left.

Final page?
It doesn't come with closure.

Just a breath -
and a question:
What will you name the next one?

- *Suraj Kumar.*

# Co-author

# Tarun Kaushik

# She's not a rose – she's more beautiful than its petals

I've never seen her face,
But I'm sure her smile could outshine the moon.
She's the first ray of the morning sun,
The fragrance of blooming flowers,
The thirst of a wandering bee,
The calm of a flowing river.

She is a longing that may never be fulfilled,
The scent of sandalwood groves…
Far away from me,
Yet always so close - right within my heart.

I walk with pain tucked inside my chest,
Gently kissing her photograph like a sacred secret.
If someone asks how I'm doing,
I simply smile.
And if they ask her name…
I whisper my own.

- *Tarun Kausik.*

# Let me live

Let me live…
Why do you keep tormenting me like this?
You hold me close,
Yet you make me cry in your arms.

Perhaps you wish I'd just die—
You must be saying it silently, every moment.

I'm used to enduring pain,
So I keep bearing it…
If tears are written in my destiny,
Then I simply keep weeping…

You've burned so many hearts,
Made so many cry in silence.
Take a moment—ask yourself someday,
Why did you betray? And for what?

Now I search for a new identity,
Trying to find myself within you.
If I wanted, I could change you for me…
But no,
I love you exactly as you are.

- *Tarun Kausik.*

# Co-author

# Vansh Sharma

Vansh Sharma is a passionate writer and a deep observer of life's emotions. At just 19, he crafts poetry that touches on love, loss, growth, and everything in between. With every line, Vansh captures raw, heartfelt truths from daily life and wraps them in relatable, meaningful expression. Apart from writing, Vansh finds peace in playing badminton, engaging in deep conversations, and reflecting on the quiet moments that make us who we are. His words often speak for those who feel too much but say too little.

# The emotions we wear

We walk through life with masks so thin,
Some stitched with joy, some soaked in sin.
A silent ache beneath each smile,
We dance in pain and rest awhile.

A mother's tear, a father's pride,
A dream once lost we keep inside.
The heart remembers every beat,
The ones we love, the ones we meet.

Laughter rings but hides the fear,
Of losing what we hold so near.
Eyes that shine with silent storms,
Smiles that never quite conform.

A friend who left, a word unsaid,
The weight we carry, the tears we've shed.
Yet through the cracks, we bloom, we rise,
With stitched-up hope and borrowed skies.

We fear, we fall, we fail, we feel -
Still search for truths no wounds can steal.
From grief to grace, from scars to light,
We learn to stand, we learn to fight.

We wear our love like second skin,
A prayer whispered deep within.
For every goodbye, there's a start,
A chapter inked upon the heart.

Emotions - raw, unfiltered, wide,
The waves we surf, the tides we hide.
The anger, calm, the trust, the doubt,
The silent screams we never shout.

But oh, how brave the soul must be,
To hold the pain and still break free.
To write of sorrow yet not sink,
To cry in lines, in every ink.

Life's story is not pure or plain,
It's stitched with gold, it's soaked in rain.
Yet every drop and every tear,
Turns into stardust we hold dear.

So pen your love, your grief, your flame,
You're more than hurt, you're more than name.
Each page you write, each breath you bear,
You show the world - the life you wear.

- *Vansh Sharma.*

# Co-author Wolfie

He is like a cactus, the closer you come to him, the more you will hurt yourselves.

## A dime for mine

As if clock was ticking for mine as if those hearts ache
for mine searched my pocket for a quarter to buy some
time but all there was just a dime.

- *Wolfie.*

## Sins

I again atone my sins
I see the bruises that I gave leaving behind trail of pain
now I'll hold the blade that harms bury the red drop from
my palm.

- *Wolfie.*

www.ingramcontent.com/pod-product-compliance
Lightning Source LLC
Chambersburg PA
CBHW031522180726
48282CB00056B/224
* 9 7 8 8 1 9 9 1 3 5 7 9 6 *